I0539073

Ribbons and Role Play

A Stepbrother Reverse Harem Romance

Ribbons and Role Play

A Stepbrother Reverse Harem Romance

Part of the

Christmas Cherry Auction series

Sylvie Haas

SYLVIE HAAS

Copyright

Contents

Blurb

Running away from my own wedding is bound to irritate everyone involved, but for once, I'm sticking up for myself.

But where to run?

On a wild hair, I head straight to the Christmas Cherry Auction.

What I don't realize is that my motorcycle club stepbrothers aren't far behind!

How much family strife am I willing to cause?

If you love dirty-talking men who know how to please their stepsister, don't miss this year's Christmas Cherry Auction!

One

Knight

The uptight, pompous prick standing at the front of the church has no idea I'm about to risk everything to ruin his day.

Neither does my little stepsister he's about to marry.

And neither does his friend, my stepdad, who's sitting to my immediate left.

Holding the jacket of my tux open, I retrieve the piece of paper that changed my path. I haven't even told my brothers about my plan—because it wasn't exactly a plan. It was a wild idea presented to me as a fortune in a cookie.

I roll my shoulders, trying to get comfortable in the required attire. My two brothers and I are more comfortable straddling a Harley than perching in a pew.

Angling my head over my shoulder to stretch my neck, I wonder if this is the wedding Wendy always dreamed of or did our parents decide. Giant, identical bundles of flowers at the end of each pew, a red carpet, and a string quartet are more of my parents' signature.

The quartet shifts to something less...classic. An instrumental version of a pop song, possibly. At least it's from this century.

Everyone shifts their attention to the back of the room. The first bridesmaid and groomsman couple start their slow walk to the front. He's as old and stuffy as the groom, who's as old as our dad. She's young and vibrant, with streaks of blue in her hair. I recognize her as one of Wendy's roller derby teammates. That blue hair is the first sign Wendy has anything to do with this formal wedding.

The whole thing—minus the blue hair—reeks of our stepdad. Always pompous and posturing. If he didn't make my mom immensely happy, I wouldn't give him the time of day.

I rub my thumb over the long, rectangular fortune and exhale hard. I'll be judged for choosing now to stand up for my stepsister. But wrecking her wedding will be minor compared to what else I want to do.

The fucker standing at the front of the church started dating her when she was seventeen and proposed to her on her eighteenth birthday. Something doesn't add up.

Not just because my sister makes my cock hard. Not just because she's marrying someone I don't trust. And not just because a tiny piece of paper convinced me to say what I've kept secret.

It's getting hot. I glance at my fist that's concealing the piece of paper. If I sweat enough to dissolve the fortune, should I forever hold my peace? I run a finger around my collar.

The second bridesmaid and groomsman enter. Add one more stuffy old dude to the room. And a pin-up girl. I recognize her from the roller derby team, too.

Wendy's a free spirit, full of zest and zeal—and other words I only think of in relation to her. Why would she commit to a man who looks like he ran out of wild oats before she was even born?

Relaxing my fingers slightly, I confirm the ink remains on the paper: *Claim your destiny with your heart, and the important things will fall into place.*

Why do these things have to be so vague?

Our stepdad stands and crosses in front of me to the side of the church. I lean forward, looking past my brothers. One of the bridesmaids has signaled Dad over. Why isn't she in back with Wendy? Her expression indicates she got shit duty to tell him that some piece of minutia didn't go as planned.

Instead of having a bridezilla at this wedding, the Father Of the Bride is the one to watch for. Would that make him FOBzilla?

The sternness in Dad's expression crushes the humor. My brother, Nova, is closest. His head whips toward us, his face has gone white, and he instantly leans his mouth to Axel's ear.

Axel quickly turns to me and whispers, "Wendy ran."

Did she just save me from having to wreck her wedding? That's not right. I should be saving her. But Nova...this hits him hard. He never speaks of it, but he was jilted years ago, and had another serious relationship go south before that.

We lean close to one another. "What do you mean, *ran*?"

"From what the chick said, Wendy signaled for the ceremony to start, then rushed back into the changing room. The procession continued, but this chick was last, so she went to check on Wendy, who was tearing off her dress. She said not to follow her, then left."

"Naked?" My cock is shamelessly hard.

"That's what you're focusing on?" Axel, our youngest brother, says.

We all look at Mr. Cooper as he returns to his seat next to me.

"We have a problem. Come with me." He stands, faces the attendees, and with complete stoicism says, "Please remain seated."

He ushers us and our mom down a side hallway. His expression has shifted from stoic to worried. The man actually cares that his daughter freaked out. He might be human after all. "One of the bridesmaids just informed me that Wendy took off."

Dad's barely finished the statement when Nova says, "We'll look for her. We can get the whole motorcycle club to help." He's regained color and jumps into action to smooth things out. How far down did he shove the pain of his two failed relationships?

Mentioning the MC around Mr. Cooper is generally a bad idea. But for once, Dad looks relieved.

"Do it. She doesn't realize what's good for her."

"Good for her?" Axel asks.

"I worked hard to make this wedding happen. We only have until Christmas to lock down the marriage, and she runs out? She's too young to know what's good for her, for her future, for the legacy I'm building."

The wedding is a business deal? Everything clicks into place. Axel's wheels are turning and Nova mutters, "Fuck." He's always stepping in to keep the peace because he avoids conflict like the plague. Will this new information change his desire to help? We've never talked about our stepsister in anything but family terms. Not as a commodity. And definitely not as a sexual entity—which is the second bomb that will be dropped today.

I have no doubt what needs to be done. I extend my hand to assure Dad that we'll find our sister, and the paper I'm holding catches his attention. He reaches for it. Shit.

It's too private to let anyone see, even though they wouldn't understand. Yanking my hand away, a ripping sound lets me know I wasn't fast enough. Half of the fortune is in his hands.

I snatch it from him too late.

"Was that from a fortune cookie? Is that where you get your advice on *destiny*?"

I shove the pieces into my jacket pocket as he shakes his head. My brothers look at me curiously.

Our stepdad continues, "Don't look for answers on a whimsical piece of paper. Try manning up and doing the hard things."

Exactly what I was about to do, but that's irrelevant now. "We'll find Wendy, Sir."

What I don't tell him is that I have no intention of bringing her back to this business deal. I can't imagine a worse life for Wendy than to be confined by a loveless marriage. She's a beautiful soul, a creative spirit, and I'll make sure she knows that when I find her.

Axel rushes ahead and confirms that Wendy's car is gone. It had been suspicious that she insisted on driving herself to the wedding. My brothers and I head outside while Dad handles the guests.

Nova says, "I texted the MC."

We make a game plan, fire up our bikes, and roll out. Thanks to technology, we stay updated on any texts about Wendy without having to stop and check our phones.

Mom and Dad had been irritated that Wendy wanted our father seated when the ceremony started instead of him walking her down the aisle. I'd attributed it to my spirited, yet slightly stubborn sister doing things their own way. Now I wonder if it was part of her exit plan.

It doesn't take long for a message to come through that one of our MC brothers spotted Wendy's car. What I'm not prepared for is that she pulled into the Aubergine Affair, a sex club that's hosting the Christmas Cherry Auction tonight. I heard about last year's auction. All of the women ended up in reverse harems.

My heart races. If she plans to auction herself, she better be prepared for me to win.

My brothers and I get there in record time, arriving one right after another.

As we're striding toward the door, I fill them in. "I'm going to buy her. I'm going to fuck her. I'll explain later."

Axel clenches his fist. "I'm in. I'll buy her with you."

Before I can clarify if he also wants the other half of what I proposed, Nova looks at us as if we've lost our minds. "Joking?"

I bark out, "Nope."

Axel answers quickly. "Me either."

"That's not right. Dad will be pissed."

We're almost to the door. "Yep, but I'm claiming my destiny tonight."

"Well...fuck." Nova shakes his head. "Destiny it is."

Are they seriously in this with me?

Two

Wendy

My virginity is not a commodity to be traded between men. My pulse pounds in my ears as I storm into the sex club, ask that I be added to the program, and join the other three ladies.

Bianca, Aurora, and Cindy are more than welcoming, even giving me a Christmas dress that will allow me to look as festive as they do—much better than my white sweats with 'BRIDE' written in silver down one leg. Aurora dusts me with body glitter. I love her for that, and I love that they don't ask too many questions.

I don't even have answers for myself. Like how did my father know I was still a virgin? And did he really think that it was appropriate to pledge my virginity as part of a business deal? If I hadn't overheard their conversation an hour before the wedding, I would have played the part of a fool—blindly believing a gazillionaire would be interested in me.

Ick.

A shiver runs up my spine...and back down...a couple of times. So creepy to hear that I was part of a contract negotiation. Scratch that. *I* wasn't the important item—the tightness of my vagina was up for sale. That's not okay. And that's way understating things.

The auction proceeds chaotically, but I barely register any of it.

I have one mission tonight—prove that virginity isn't a big deal. Sex isn't a big deal. The only reason I haven't had sex is that the moment, or rather the guy, never seemed right. I didn't want to have a crappy get-it-over-with first time.

Based on last year's auction, this is the perfect place to get my cherry popped while not worrying that I'll end up with a crappy memory instead of orgasms.

I don't want to admit that this plan has niggled in my brain for days, and I definitely don't want to admit that the glimmer of it started weeks ago.

In retrospect it all makes sense—the little comments and awkward moments that started as soon as I accepted his marriage proposal three months ago. A switch flipped. Hints that he thought he owned me morphed from fun to troublesome.

When the bridesmaids lined up, and the music shifted to one of the only choices I got to make in my own wedding, fear of my future finally screamed loud enough for me to trust myself.

Ironically, the only thing scarier than the life my father had set out for me, is not having his support and his certainty. I've lived a precious life because of the legacy he's creating.

But I didn't understand I had to pay for it. I can't imagine how furious he is.

A ruckus disrupts the auction and a faint rumble of motorcycles filters backstage. Cindy and I sort out that Aurora's brothers are demanding she go with them. But my brothers enter, and I might have a bigger problem.

Are they going to drag me back to my wedding before I have a chance to complete my mission? They don't like my father but they respect him. They would follow his orders to save the day.

The world is a blur as I step onto the stage. I'm aware that all of the other women were bought by their stepbrothers. If they get to live in a fantasy world, is it too much to ask that I live there too?

All of the hope that's ever existed wells in my heart when the bidding starts. My brothers bid on me as a group. Knight is the one raising the paddle. The look of sheer determination on his face and the glare he gives anyone else who bids on me, leave me uncertain as to his motivation.

Nova's expression is softer as always. It's through the ease on his face that I sense they're not going to take me back to the wedding.

And Axel? He would have come backstage and told me we had to leave. He doesn't tolerate nonsense.

But if they're not here to take me back, why are they here?

The auctioneer seems to be calling for a million dollars and other paddles continue lifting into the air. Knight's lifting motion grows firmer each time. His scowl deeper.

Are they bidding to protect me, or... I almost hate to let Fantasy Wendy run wild...bidding to *win* me.

Is it foolish to ask my stepbrothers to claim my virginity?

"Two million," Knight growls. I've never heard him like that. Never seen the dark possessiveness as he looks to the stage. Never wanted him so badly, and that says a lot because Fantasy Wendy has a lot of fun with her brothers and a vibrator.

The auctioneer stops.

Knight continues, "I'm not about to let any of you assholes get your hands on my des—" His words cut off then he resumes. "my stepsister."

The grumbling amongst the attendees rattles around incomprehensibly in my head. It's the statement from the auctioneer that makes it through. "Two million! Going...going...sold!"

I make a mad dash off stage and switch back into my clothes so nothing happens to Aurora's dress. I already ruined one dress today. And if I have to face my father, I'd rather not have to explain where I've been.

"Come with me." Knight is storming toward me when I step back onto the stage.

With clarity, I say, "I'm not going back to the wedding."

"I'm not taking you back to the wedding."

"I came here for one reason. I have to have sex tonight. I have to take away Dad's power to use me like property."

"What the fuck?" Knight says as our brothers catch up to him.

"My virginity was part of a business deal."

They all look shocked, but Knight sets a hand on my shoulder. The contact is comforting and seductive. His jaw clenches. "I didn't know it was a business deal until after you left. And I didn't know—"

"No reason you would know about my sex life. And I didn't know about the business deal until right before the wedding."

"Your goal is to have sex tonight?" Knight's voice catches.

"Yes," I say more firmly than I feel.

He turns to the people who haven't left yet. "Get out of here unless you want to see me fuck my stepsister."

Fantasy Wendy isn't going to have to do all of the work tonight, but I'm not sure a public announcement is the right approach. Father will be humiliated if his children have sex. Serves him right.

Three

Wendy

Knight trails his fingers down my braid. "It was risky of you to do this."

The intimate gesture is prolonged as he toys with the white ribbon securing the bottom.

I want to say the right things to ensure Knight will help me. Can he see my reasoning? "Auctioning myself for sex didn't seem so bad in comparison to actually being sold. One night, four hours, however you want to look at it."

His hand shifts and he tugs my braid, tipping my face up. His deep blue eyes storm with thoughts. "You have no idea who could have bought you."

"Then I guess I got lucky."

Nova steps close. "I'm sorry Dad treated you like that. I would've helped sooner if I'd known. Promise me you won't ever pull a stunt like this again. Come to us if you have a problem."

"If you help me tonight, I won't have this problem again." I suspect Knight is most likely to be willing to have sex with me, but Fantasy Wendy leaves our options open.

Nova's jaw strains. Axel joins us but remains caught in his head. Their combined body heat and musky scents do a number on me.

I take advantage of the pause. "I've thought this out. Let's keep it impersonal, just to get the job done. I won't even take my shirt off."

"Oh, no, Baby Doll, that's not how this works."

I hold a finger up. "Are you missing the point? I'm not having men dictate my life. You heard my offer, take it or leave it."

Which is completely contrary to my body's reaction to the nickname.

Knight lets his hand trail from my braid to my shoulder, down my back, and I'm ridiculously swoony at the sensation of his strong hand guiding me from behind. "Get in this room."

"We should go home."

"We're doing it right here. Right now. You want to prove that your virginity is gone. You're going to need witnesses."

"But..."

"No buts. I plan on giving you exactly what you want; proof that you've had sex." He has a point. Not everyone was deterred by his statement that he was about to fuck his stepsister. Several people have gathered around.

Inside the dimly lit room, I give one last thought to closing the curtains in front of the glass wall to block the view for those still present. Fantasy Wendy turns my attention to a leather padded bench that's about waist height. I lean over the bench, unsure what the ideal height would be.

Whatever it is, the warmth of Knight's hand caressing my clothed ass makes this height perfect. My body betrays me with a shudder. His other hand reaches up, tugs on the ribbon in my hair again, and forces my head to the side.

Pull harder. Fantasy Wendy makes a note. *Hair pulling. Check. Love it.*

Nova steps beside me. "Are you sure you want it like this?"

"Yes." I gulp down my answer.

Knight spins me to face him. His thick fingers tuck into the waistband of my white sweatpants. The glittery 'BRIDE' label I'd been so eager to earn might as well have spelled out 'PROPERTY'. How will I ever trust a man again? How will I trust myself?

He kneels, slowly and reverently. The lowering of my sweatpants over my hips removes the once-exciting label, revealing my white satin panties.

Knight abandons my sweats just above my knees. Awkward.

He's staring. Even more awkward. Should I ask one of my other brothers to do the deed?

Knight's hands wrap around my hips, stopping words from being able to leave my mouth. His firm, intimate grip has

Fantasy Wendy screaming from the cage I've locked her in. *Let us out. Let us have a chance at reality.*

Yeah...no. I'm not stupid. This is a transaction. We'll have sex. I'll no longer be a virgin. And by the grace of escaping my wedding, I belong to no one but myself.

Fantasy Wendy objects. I give her a lollipop and tell her to sit quietly in her cage. Her obedience is vital for me to maintain my façade of indifference. Getting attached to a man, or men, is not tonight's plan. Not a plan I can ever have with my stepbrothers. They are strictly fantasy fodder.

Knight slides one thumb forward, stroking the front of my panties, and pauses on the two tiny rings held by a bow.

Guys are so out of touch with pretty things. He leans forward, pausing an inch in front of my sex. I take in a breath since I seem to have stopped breathing.

Why the staring? Why aren't we having sex? Why does the warmth of his breath send pulses of excitement through me? Can warm breaths actually melt my legs? I'm on the verge of not being able to support—

He closes the gap. He bites the bow and rings. My panties are caught in his mouth as he yanks his head back and to the side.

A ripping sound is followed by the slap of my panties back into me. I'm staring now as he spits the tiny jewelry onto the floor. The once-decorative white ribbon and miniature gold bands clink as they hit the dark marble then skid another few inches.

He growls before looking up at me. "That prick doesn't deserve to be anywhere near you."

"I know." I'm not sure the words exit my mouth.

"This isn't the way your first time should be."

Fantasy Wendy clanks her lollipop over the bars of her imprisonment like a felon. Why am I having to dig so deep to keep my façade in place? I take control.

Fantasy Wendy, your judgment can't be trusted. You believed a man thirty years older than you could be our true love. That he could actually be interested in an eighteen-year-old roller derby, graphic artist. Our heart is on lockdown until further notice.

Thanks to my imagination, I shove the lollipop back into her mouth and divert my eyes from Knight kneeling in front of me. Shifting my attention across my selection of stepbrothers, I say, "If you're not up for it, I'll find someone who is. But never fear, I'll make good on the four hours of holiday help you won in the auction."

I'm so busy applauding myself, I don't register what's happening until it's over. Knight grabbed my panties on both sides and ripped them from my body.

Fantasy Wendy drops her lollipop. I'm pretty sure she's drooling, but Knight has my attention.

"Fuck the auction, then fuck me." His voice is low and possessive. He stands and unzips his pants. I hand Fantasy Wendy her lollipop so she has something to suck on. It's not like I haven't seen a penis before. I just haven't seen one that makes me want to drop to my knees while simultaneously riding it. Sure, it's physically impossible, but my eyes flit to Axel and Nova. We could improvise.

What is wrong with me? And why is my brother letting me stare when I return my eyes to him? Nope. This isn't a four-hour porn session. I just need to lose my freaking virginity. Tab A. Slot B. Let's go.

I turn around, bending over the bench. His tip prodding at my sopping wet entrance might as well be a cattle prod. Electricity zings through my entire body. His pressure is enough to shove my body forward into the bench, but not enough to enter me.

My core knots with an insane intensity. Way better than my vibrator.

I shove my hips back, forcing his tip into me a tiny bit. My lips strain and stretch around him. The sharp sting is eclipsed by his groans and the pain of his fingers digging into my hips. The pain is nothing worse than I put up with in roller derby, and the good parts are way better.

I can't believe it. I'm having sex for the first time. I'm officially not a virgin. I want to have a party. I want to scream it in my father's face—to the world, that virginity is a stupid way to gauge a woman's worth, but all I can think about is how much I need the rest of Knight's cock inside of me.

I use the bench for leverage as Knight pumps slow and hard behind me. One of his hands returns to my hair, fisting a braid, pulling my head back. My entire body is alive. I wish I'd taken my clothes off. My nipples are beaded so hard, I can feel them dragging across the bench through my bra and shirt. I want to feel his entire body the way I feel his cock. I want to slide over him, our skin slick with perspiration.

I *need* this to end as quickly as possible. That's going to be easy. I'm plunging wickedly fast toward the abyss of release. The moment I lose control, a rhythmic pulsing of my sex tightens and relaxes around his shaft. His hand slides from my hair onto my shoulder, and he drives himself into me, thrusting hard and fast.

The throbbing of his cock matches the growls pouring from him, and is followed by the warmth of his release streaming down my legs, then the warmth of his body leaning over me. I could get used to this.

No! Fantasy Wendy, get back in your cage.

His still-hard cock makes it hard for me to think rationally. I need to end this. We're not here to cuddle. Movement catches my attention and helps a few brain cells fire up. I'd forgotten all about the people watching.

One man has his arms wrapped around a woman. His fingers are tucked between her legs, and based on her mouth hanging open... Oh my gosh! I'm watching her orgasm. It gets my insides ready to go again.

Shoot. This isn't going right. I need to get out of here before I jump all of my brothers.

"Thank you." I find the words tumbling from my lips as his cock twitches inside of me. "Mission accomplished."

Normally my awkwardness would distract the people around me, give me a chance to escape, but Knight wraps his arms around my waist, keeping his lips at my ear.

"Don't call this a mission and don't call it accomplished."

"Well, it is. I needed to have sex."

"And you can keep having it." Why does his low voice make me warm inside?

"No need. We've already overachieved. Made sure there were witnesses."

He slides his cock from me and Nova offers his pocket square. It's like using a tissue to clean a gallon of spilled milk, but I try.

"Wendy, I don't want this to end."

My name on Knight's lips makes the moment oddly personal.

"It has to, Knight. You're my brother."

"Your *step*brother."

Four

Wendy

None of us knew how to handle what happened last night. Under the 'mission accomplished' pretense, I went home. Thankfully, I'd moved out of my dad's house, but I paid for my little house with his money.

I would take comfort in having a job, but it's at my dad's company. The family that once offered me security has a stranglehold on my life.

Without a honeymoon to rush off to and no desire to use my ticket in case my supposed-to-be husband decides to use his, I go to morning roller derby practice. At the very least I need to field the questions my bridesmaids will have about the wedding.

I only turned my phone on to let the team know I was coming. In one fell swoop, I dismissed all of the messages that piled up overnight. I texted Mom and Dad, asking them to take a few days to consider my position, and told them I'd be in touch. Then I blocked them.

I arrive at the skate rink and my phone rings. I turn the volume down.

Barely inside the door, Nikki, the bridesmaid I'd given the terrible task of notifying my father, catches me. "Hey, are you all right, Wendy?"

"I'm sorry I bailed. I had to escape."

I let my gear bag thunk on the ground and sit on the long wooden bench. I toss my phone in my bag, ignoring it vibrating. She joins me in lacing our skates.

"What happened?" Nikki asks. She glances toward my buzzing bag and I wave it off.

It's good that she doesn't know since she works at my dad's company. It means the rumor mill hasn't explained that I let my stepbrother claim my virginity in front of people at the sex club. Supposedly they take privacy breaches very seriously, but we all know what money can do.

"I was being married off as part of a business deal. Every time he said *I love you,* he meant he loved money and power. I was just the tool to secure it."

"No shit." Nikki's fingers stop moving, leaving her laces dangling.

"Yeah. Part of the drawback to having an uber-powerful father— He thinks he can do things like that."

"That sucks," another teammate, Beatrix says from nearby.

"But you got out of it, right? You're not in an arranged marriage?" Nikki asks.

"For now." I stand and adjust my spandex shorts, avoiding explaining the whole virginity thing. "I just want to get my life back."

Nikki slaps me on the ass. "Yeah. Come on. Let's..."

My phone buzzes from inside my bag again.

"Maybe you should check that," Nikki says. "We'll start skating laps. No one expects you to be ready today."

I unzip my bag, curious who it could be. It's Knight: *We're not done with you*

I type back: *We?*

Like an idiot, after I send the message, I see that Axel and Nova are in the group chat. Not that there was much question.

Knight: *I'm not done with you*

Axel: *If you need to be extra sure you're not a virgin, I can help*

Me: *I'm pretty sure it's one-and-done*

I'm cracking up at this text exchange. No use reading anything into Nova not responding.

Knight: *We have an offer for you*

Me: ???

I'm fairly certain Fantasy Wendy got control of my fingers. There's no rational reason I would have a text exchange with my brothers about sex.

The phone rings and it's a number I don't know. I'm not in the mood to talk to a stranger but my finger accidentally taps the answer button instead of Reject Call. Gah! I cautiously lift it to my ear.

"Hello?"

"What the hell were you thinking, Wendy?" It's Dad. Not sure who's phone he's calling from. My heart sinks as I watch my friends skate around the track smiling, laughing, sling-shotting each other in practice moves.

"I said I'd be in touch in a few days. I'll be at work Monday." My head drops backward. Ugh!

"No need. If you can't respect the importance of this wedding, you're fired."

I snap upright. It's not that I don't respect authority. It's that I don't respect it blindly. But I know how Dad is. There's no point arguing. I'm no more than an employee who messed up a giant contract.

I offer a simple, "Okay," then drop my phone in my bag and push off to join my girlfriends in the rink. They're my found family. They accept me for who I am. I don't get treated special here. I'm not the girl with all the money and the legacy. I'm just a girl who's willing to skate and shove people around and have a really good time.

The thoughts in my mind settle as I skate warmup laps. My dad didn't mention sex, just the wedding. Surely he would've mentioned my public stepbrother fucking if he knew.

Fantasy Wendy tries to get me to leave the rink and text my brothers to see what their offer is. I almost agree.

But, it would be a family disaster. One screwup of a child is almost expected, but two...three...four. That's too much. I have to end this nonsense. I'll deal with that later, though, when I can take time to leave a clear message—this is my life and no one is going to control me.

The tough façade I put on last night needs to become my daily wear until this passes.

In truth, I want love and support. I want people that I can lean on. That's what the roller derby team is. Roller derby's also a great place to get my frustrations out and let my inner badass shine.

Five

Nova

"I don't disagree with you, Knight." I shove dishes in the dishwasher instead of joining my brothers in texting Wendy.

Knight slams a pile of papers onto the kitchen counter as he sort of straightens them. "Then what the fuck is it, Nova? You're either in or out. Don't confuse her. And don't fucking pout when Axel and I rope her in without you."

"I'm in. I want her."

"Then send a text. Let her know." Axel grabs an energy drink from the fridge then slams the door shut. "We have to be clear."

I can't get out of my head. None of us has had a successful relationship, thus why we're all single. But I've given my heart away twice—in the form of diamond engagement rings. Once, I made it to the altar. My fiancée didn't.

Knight adds, "Wendy's unsettled. She's young. Our father manipulated her. We can't have her thinking we'll do the same. We have to go in strong and show that we can take care of her."

"Yeah, I get it."

Axel pops the top on his can. "I can see you might be worried after...your past. Don't let it fuck this up."

I can't keep up with them. "She was a runaway bride yesterday. What makes you think she's ready to shack up with three guys she's never dated? Oh yeah, she hasn't dated them because they're her brothers. Do you hear how insane this is?" I shut the water off and sort a handful of silverware into the basket. "Besides, you had sex with her in front of us and other people. That's not the kind of relationship I want."

"How would you know? You haven't been with a woman in how long?" Knight's harsh about my situation. He's also wrong. I've never been *with* a woman, which makes this all the more awkward. If we were teens, sticking my dick in my stepsister would be one thing, but now?

My cock volunteers to give it a shot. I turn back to the sink so my brothers can't see. Wendy's everything I love in a woman. Feisty and free. But she's our stepsister. How does that not bug them?

"We're not talking about having sex in public all the time," Axel says. He's so private, it would shock me if he ever did, but they're acting crazy about Wendy. "This would be a thing between the four of us."

"Have you two shared before?" I ask them.

"No, but there's something special about Wendy. We'll give her a choice, but we'd rather share her than lose her to someone else. Axel would be a pillar of stability and practicality for her. I would be the one to make sure she's pampered. And you could round it out, always keep things peaceful for her? We each have something to offer beyond our cocks."

I'm seeing red as the conversation opens too many wounds. Turning the tables, I ask, "Keeping things peaceful? Did I do a good job of that when my fiancée got a boyfriend? Did I handle it smoothly when my bride *didn't* walk down the aisle? Is this the trifecta to round it out? Guarantee I'll face another…"

I turn the water on and run the garbage disposal to drown everything out. How can they think this will be anything more than having a fuck fest with our sister? Will any of us survive the adventure? Will we take our entire family down? Have we already?

Our phones buzz and there's a message from our stepdad. The man's a fucking mind reader.

Dad: *Cut off all communication with Wendy*

What the fuck? I read it then lift my gaze to see what my brothers think. Knight is rubbing his chest and Axel just stares aimlessly at his phone.

"How do you plan on dealing with him?" I ask.

Knight tosses his phone on the counter. "We can deal with *him* or we can deal with *her*. I know which side I'm taking."

"He'll find out you fucked her. How eager are you to make it worse?"

Axel explains, "We'll talk to her, see if she feels the same, but I can't see a future without her. I've never hated anything as much as attending her wedding. I couldn't understand why one of Dad's business partners would show so much interest in her then pounce on her with a marriage proposal at her eighteenth birthday party. I can't believe I didn't see it."

"I'm in the same boat as Axel, Nova. I can't explain how, but I know I'm supposed to be with her. What do we have to lose?"

"We're putting our future in the hands of an eighteen-year-old roller derby girl. Do you think we don't have something to lose?" My voice raises. I never knew my brothers felt this way about Wendy. They're saying all of the things I've denied. I swore I'd never fall in love again, but Wendy...she threatens my control daily.

Knight slams his fist on the counter hard enough that his phone bounces. "Quit saying you're in then making excuses."

They've got me cornered. My heart is too fragile to handle another breakup. But watching them be with her and not participating, would destroy my relationship with them.

"I need to talk to her." I don't have a fucking clue what I'm going to say, I just need to get away from this conversation.

Six

Wendy

After a physically exhausting derby practice, I fear being inside my house alone. I want a shoulder to cry on. I want to feel loved. I want to see my stepbrothers. Should I check with them to see what their offer is?

Gasoline meet fire.

I tried watching some self-help gurus last night and they suggested that sitting alone with yourself can be the hardest thing to do. It can also be the most cathartic if you use the time to get to know yourself rather than wallow in your pain. I can try. I can also update my resume and search for a job.

Turning onto my street, something isn't right. A car is in my driveway. It belongs to Knight.

The endorphin rush from practice fades as fear niggles through my mind. Were their texts a trick? Did Dad tell them to bring me in? That's exactly something he would do. Or are they here to break my resolve?

My futile effort at losing my virginity probably doesn't even matter to Dad's business partner. I refuse to acknowledge the man by his name, all he'll ever be is my dad's business partner. I've had enough time to realize the loyalty created by marrying our two families is the real selling point. My virginity was merely a bonus feature, or maybe an upsell. Would you like fries with that?

So basically, I fucked my brother at a sex club to keep someone from getting fries with their burger. Very mature.

I might as well get this over with. My brothers get out of their car when I turn into the driveway. I pull past them and park in the garage. It gives me a brief moment to fortify myself.

Heading to my door, I say, "We're done." I wave them off as they follow me. "I'm not interested in whatever you have to say."

"We think you might be," Knight says.

"Are you here because Dad told you to be?"

"On the contrary, he told us not to communicate with you."

"Then you should probably listen to him." Isn't that interesting? My dad and I agree on something.

Nova says, "We just want to talk. And since you backed out of your wedding and then auctioned yourself, we're guessing you need someone to talk to."

I direct my lie to Knight while fumbling the keys at the front door. "Are you going to get all needy? It was just sex."

Knight steps behind me, his fingers wrapping around my pigtail. He gives it a little tug, A shiver betrays how much I like it.

"Was it?" he whispers beside my head.

I drop my keys. Dammit. I turn sideways, bumping him, and thankfully he gives me space to pick them up. I focus on sliding the key in the lock, which ends up teasing my sex as I remember how good it felt when he moved inside of me.

"It was sex, mission accomplished remember?" I need to convince all of us.

"That's what you said, but your body told me something else. Let us in so we can talk."

There are so many penalty whistles and red flags going off in my mind, but my free spirit convinces me that inviting my brothers inside is nothing compared to running from my wedding.

If they were carting me back to dad, they would have shoved me in the car already.

What's the worst that can happen? I take Axel up on confirming that my virginity is gone?

They decline drinks and find places to sit in my living room, which is decidedly small with the three of them.

Knight goes first. "Would you consider a relationship with us?"

Whoa. Us? I play it cool while trying to figure them out. "I wouldn't know how to pick."

"We're not asking you to pick."

Nova wrings his hands and is the only one of them not staring at me.

Axel says, "We're sure you're fully aware of other sibling groups and unusual relationships in the area."

Words fail me because if I admit this, I'm admitting so much more, so many hidden desires. But getting out from under my father's thumb, only to submit to my three brothers? Is that what Real-World Wendy wants? Fantasy Wendy is banned from voting.

"I am aware of them. I just don't think it can work for us." I lower my eyes. "I already got fired for running away from my wedding. If we..." I motion between all of us. "If any of us become a thing, Dad will hold it against whoever's involved. I can't take you down on my sinking ship."

Knight says, "If you're on a sinking ship, I want to be by your side to save you from drowning."

I glance at Nova and Axel. They both nod.

Axel says, "We can pull this off. We can keep it between us at first, test drive the relationship before any reveal. We want to be on it with you."

The last thing I want is a relationship but Fantasy Wendy seems to have found a way to ball gag me when I open my mouth. I reach a compromise with her so I can do more than stand there gaping.

She allows me to ask, "How can you know you want a relationship with me?"

Knight says, "It's hard to explain."

"Yeah, like trying to explain flight to a snail."

Axel laughs. "You're hardly a snail, but I've always thought there was something special about you. I kept it quiet, a taboo thought, wanting my stepsister. But watching Knight fuck you, my future has never been so clear. I need you."

Need? Fantasy Wendy loves Axel's word choice. I attempt to dial it back. "You want to have sex with me."

"I didn't mean it like that. I feel a sense of freedom when I'm with you. I don't get as caught in my head when I have a conversation with you. It's easy to be with you. I've never felt that with anyone. I'm a better person with you."

Axel makes me feel safe. He thinks everything out. Is considerate of his words. And I make him better? No. "You're a good person period."

"I have to disagree. I want a life with you so I can be the man I was meant to be."

That's too much. "You want non-sexual things?"

"Yes."

"Name one."

Without missing a beat, he says, "I want you to come on the toy run with us. We go to a bunch of locations that have been collecting toys, stopping briefly at each one so kids can come out and look at our bikes. Then we ride off with our big red Santa bags. Back at the clubhouse, we sort, wrap, and organize the toys for delivery."

"But Dad said not to talk to me. If he finds out, he'll be furious."

"He can't be furious that you helped with a children's charity event. The media coverage is huge. Always a win for our family."

"A win for the children," I correct.

"Right, but all Dad sees is how good it is for the family image. He'll get the fuck over it."

No longer trusting my judgment, I can't tell if this is an example of poking the bear, or an effort to remind Dad we're still a family. "Okay, let's do it."

Seven

Knight

We pick Wendy up at her place. I called dibs to drive her from her house to our starting point, but I'm not sure I remember how to ride a motorcycle. The hints of white leggings in the gap between her black, thigh-high boots and her dress make it hard for me to think.

If she's cold on the ride, I'll have to rub on all of her cold parts. What the fuck? I sound like a perv.

Seating myself between her legs, my inability to think escalates. The pressure of her legs splayed around me, knowing that her pussy is open, has me ready to spin her into my lap so I can sink inside of her.

My innocent little stepsister has ruined me, even with the fast and impersonal sex she insisted on. It's killing me not to have sex with her again so I can take my time making love to her. More important than what I want though is what she wants...space.

She's had enough of men negotiating her pussy lately. My stomach turns every time I think of our father writing her into a contract.

If time will help her accept us, I'll give it to her. Axel was a genius to invite her to the toy run.

I hate that she's going to be on the back of Axel's bike when we drive to the second location, and Nova's bike on the way to the third, but she's the best addition we've ever made to our toy run.

The kids are enamored with her. She helps them on and off the bikes. She corrals the little ones with ease, getting them to line up for pictures with the row of Harleys. She has a good eye for staging.

Our father is a dumbass for firing her. She's the best graphic designer the corporation has, even without formal training. She's going to school so she can up her game even more, but she already eclipses the other employees.

Visual organization isn't the skill I want to help her develop. That's just the thought I allow myself to have.

The thought I'm tamping down because it would get me arrested for public indecency is my desire to fuck her right here. Watching her light up as she talks to the kids, I'm ready to pump her full of babies. I hope I already have.

The Aubergine Affair normally has a birth control policy, but since the auction wasn't actually for sex, the policy was waved. I didn't bring it up because I wanted to get her pregnant. That has to be a pipe dream. Surely she wouldn't have been willing to let any winner get her pregnant.

Her cheeks get rosier as the night goes on and I fall a little more in love with her at each stop. She's as cheerful with the last kid as the first. She was made to be a mother.

When we get back to the clubhouse, Axel grabs a mug and packet of hot chocolate and preps it for her. When I pour shots of whiskey for the rest of us, she says, "Hold on a second. I like cocoa, but why don't I get that?"

"Because you're underage." And you might be pregnant, but thankfully I shut my mouth before saying the last part.

"After what we did at the sex club, you're going to call me out on that?"

"I have my reasons," Axel says.

She relents with a pout, then sips her cocoa, her tongue darting out to lick the chocolate from her lips. My cock's hard again. I really need to get a grip on this. Would this be the drawback to being with her? I'll walk around with an eternal boner? That's acceptable.

Other MC members continue bringing bags in from the back of the truck that we took around with us. While It's a good visual to have us riding with huge Santa bags on our bikes, we pick up too many toys to handle all of them.

The four of us sit in a side room. Somebody left cards and dice on the table but that's not how I want to pass the time with her. Wendy has both hands cupped around the mug, and I wrap my fingers around hers.

"Hey, Nova, go turn up the heater."

She says, "It's okay. I'll be warm in a second."

Nova heads to the thermostat. "I'd rather you be comfortable now."

I want to hear her talk about the kids. "Did you have fun tonight?"

"Yeah. I can't believe how many toys you picked up. I've heard about your toy run before, but I didn't realize how big it is."

Axel mumbles, "That's what she said."

I sure as hell hope Wendy didn't hear him but she snickers. At least the overused joke didn't offend her.

"Now it's time to sort the gifts." I hop up and grab a notebook from the cabinet. Flipping it open in front of her, I explain, "Here are all the kids, their ages, and types of things they're into. We usually do a pretty damn good job pairing the stuff we collect with individual interest, if I say so myself."

Nova adds, "It's easy to pick out the kids who like fantasy and make sure to give them the toys that fit that. The kids who are thinkers get the more educational stuff. The kids who need creative outlets get the artistic items. It's fun, and if we get it wrong, a kid might try something new and find out they like it."

"Are you glad you're trying something new, Wendy?" I ask her as I tighten my hold on her hand.

"I'm glad I went on the toy run. But..." She pulls her hands into her lap.

Dammit, with a simple question, I pushed too far. "Thank you for going with us. I didn't mean to pressure you."

"I don't want to lead you on. I'm not looking for a commitment. I still haven't fully processed that I've been groomed my whole life to belong to a man."

"We're not asking for a commitment."

Axel clears his throat.

"I take that back. We would love to commit." And if I put a baby in her already, I've secured my commitment. Fuck. Does that make me the worst brother ever? I want to make a family with her so badly, I avoided the birth control conversation. But so did she.

Wendy toys with the dice and I notice they have sex words instead of dots. She furrows her brow and reads them. A smile is short-lived when she says, "I know a lot of women are playing wife to more than one man and it's working for them. I just don't know if it's my role."

"You know how you find out if you're right for a role?" I ask.

She narrows her gaze at me.

"You audition."

Her smile returns half-heartedly. "I don't think it works that way for relationships."

Nova looks nervous but Axel catches on. "Why not? Have fun with it. Roll those dice. Audition us."

"Don't we need to sort gifts?" She taps on the open page in the notebook.

"We have all day tomorrow to sort these gifts, plus the rest of the MC helps. We can have a little fun tonight."

She rolls the dice, then her eyes get big.

One die reads, "eat pussy." The other reads, "on the table."

"I'll audition for that role." Axel shoves his chair out from the table, takes her hand, and guides her to standing. They stare into each other's eyes.

He wraps his hands around her waist and sits her on the table, her skirt flaring out around her. He kneels, unzipping one thigh-high boot, removing it, and massaging her foot before doing the same with the other boot.

"Hop down for a second, Princess." Appropriate nickname for his kneeling position.

She stands, and he reaches his hands under her skirt. In seconds her tights are thrown across the floor. I consider grabbing them and sniffing that sweet scent of her pussy, the one that lingered on my cock that I could smell each time I jacked off the other night, but I'm too captivated to move.

He pulls her head forward to kiss her. Their lip lock is epic. They work together in perfect synchronicity. Damn, I'm jealous I didn't have that. The way they're staring into each other's eyes while their tongues mingle strikes me as more intimate than getting to put my dick inside of her from behind.

Then he pulls away and says, "You ready to do what the dice say, Princess?"

"Is there anything I need to do to get ready? I've never had a guy do that?"

Oh, sweet Jesus. We're giving her all of her firsts. That's the only positive thing I've been able to find about the 'just business' marriage. He didn't get anywhere with her.

"Just spread these sweet legs." Axel grabs just below her knees and lifts her feet onto the table as she reclines. "All you have to do is relax and let me make you come."

The sound of his mouth on her pussy is the hottest thing I've heard, second to my cock sliding in and out of her. I'd been shocked by how wet she was. I swear to God her sex juice is honey because my mind is absolutely stuck on her sweetness.

I kick my chair out of the way and stand beside the table, stroking my fingers through her hair. I want her to see me when she comes. I want her to think about yesterday.

"You like that, Baby Doll?" I get her to look at me.

"Yes."

"I bet you'd like it if my cock was inside of you while he licked your clit."

She moans. She definitely didn't object. Nova leans forward on the other side of the table. He's taken a keen interest, splitting his attention between watching Axel eat pussy and the ecstasy on Wendy's face.

Axel moves a hand to her belly. I'm tempted to get my dick out and spray her belly with cum. He could rub it in for me. She's going to look so good when her belly's rounded with my baby.

Then her eyes roll back, her moans escalate, and her hand slaps out, grabbing my forearm. Her fingernails dig in. I hope she leaves her mark on me. She's doing the same to Nova on the other side. Then she splinters apart.

Her body falls limp, her chest heaving as Axel eases his drenched face away from her sex. He rubs a hand over his mustache and beard, inhaling deeply.

"Let me do that to you every day, Princess."

"Uh-huh," she says.

I'm going to take that as a commitment.

Nova's shoulders are bunched up ever so slightly. He keeps shifting from one foot to the other. I get that he has commitment issues, but how can he resist Wendy?

He bites his lower lip and is a little too fidgety with the way he holds her hand. What's going on with him?

Eight

Nova

"No commitment, right?" I tread lightly before making my big admission. I'm worried that if I wait, I'll miss my chance. The evil glare I get from Knight tells me he doesn't approve.

"Yeah," Wendy says, sitting up and sipping her cocoa.

"I need to tell you something." There's not a breath deep enough to make me feel ready for this.

"Okay," she says, but they're all staring at me.

I blurt out my secret. "I've never had sex."

She spews cocoa onto my shirt and the floor. "Oh my God, I'm sorry." She starts to jump up, but I hold her in place.

The shock on Knight's and Axel's faces is what I expected. "Keep your comments to yourselves, guys."

I turn to her. "Let one of them clean the floor. Here's the deal. I'm not ready for a relationship. You're not ready for a relationship, but I want to give this a try."

She shakes her head. "Your nickname is Nova but I remember it used to be Casanova. I assumed..."

"Just how guys razz each other. Casanova because I gave my heart away too easily. They reduced it to Nova as a joke. A loose translation to 'no go' in Spanish, since I quit dating." I rub my thumb over her lips. "But I want to explore this with you."

She grabs my wrist, kisses my thumb, and it's the best confirmation she can give me. "Do you want me to roll the dice?"

"No dice needed. I know what I want." I reach around her, unzipping her dress.

"No commitment." She unfastens my belt.

"Why set ourselves up for failure? Relationships never work." I lift the dress over her head.

The way she lifts her arms, and the little wiggle she does is almost enough to send me over the edge. Her hands sliding over my strained underwear are no help.

"And a relationship like this... Our family would never approve." She tackles my shirt, and while I'm happy to be one step closer to naked with her, I miss her touch on my cock.

I unfasten her bra. "Which is why we have to keep this a secret. Unless we're sure..." Damn her tits are perfect. I hold them in my hands, dragging my thumbs over her tight rosy nubs.

She works the waistband of my underwear over my erection and pushes them down. "Which is why you have to audition. We might try it out and decide it's not for us."

I don't think that's going to be the problem, but I can't bring myself to say it. I just don't understand how I could give my heart away to women who didn't want it. I guide her to the counter.

"Perfect. I can just lean over this. It keeps it not personal, that's what I read on the blogs."

Blogs? I spin her around. "You're not getting away with that shit." I plop her onto the counter, her ass smacking against the Formica, and scoot her to the very edge.

"The blogs also suggested dirty talk. Can we try that?"

"That one's fine. But you have to face me so I can watch you come." With my cock pressed between us, I lean in and kiss her lips. It was so fucking hot watching Axel kiss her, just like watching Knight fuck her, and now I get to do both at the same time.

I line my cock up, pressing into her sweet pussy lips. They barely make room for me. Her legs are spread wide, her hands run up and down my arms. This is going to be harder than I thought.

Every time I woke up last night, and then several times today, I yanked one out, trying to prime myself. But her scent is a sugared version of crack, and her big eyes looking up at me, and those lips that are red and swollen from our kiss. I can barely hang on.

"I'm ready for your big fat cock to fill me," she says.

For fuck's sake, she went for gold with the dirty talk. I close my eyes to eliminate the visual, and I quit breathing to cut off her scent. I even try to pull back and wrap my fist around my cock to gain control, but I can't. My balls blow load after load onto her.

I force my eyes open so I can watch. One white splat after another coats the dark curls of her pussy, her ivory skin, the countertop. Shit, I shot some on the backsplash and some up on the cabinets. She laughs and her tits bounce, giving me a moving target. I hit those too, streaking her rosy nipples with white stripes.

Fuck. The laughter starts behind me. They're never going to let me live this down.

Nine

Wendy

"Thanks for picking up this extra shift, Wendy. Now that the line's down, I may take off," Liz says then escorts a brother and sister away from Santa. She was one of my bridesmaids.

With a sudden lack of employment, I'll pick up all the extra shifts I can get. I tweaked my resume and spent a few more hours applying for jobs this morning. Or maybe it was a few minutes. Even now, as I think of last night, my hand migrates to my belly. I stop it before it dips lower.

My 'no commitment' approach is faltering at the hands of my stepbrothers.

I motion to the next family in line. "Your turn."

The mom has a baby in her arms and a little girl by her side. They're adorable. She holds her finger up. "Hang on a second. I was holding a place for someone." She turns to the side. "It's your turn, Sir."

Forcing my hand from my belly, I question the insanity of my rebellion. Running away from my wedding was self-preservation. Having unprotected sex with my stepbrothers is fate-sealing. My father would say I'm still a foolish, invincible teenager in need of guidance from wise men like him...and his business partner.

Can I get a vomit emoji? Oops, bad choice. I chuckle to myself. Vomiting after unprotected sex would indicate something I can't believe I risked. I was so caught up in the moment and the safety of my brothers, that my mind went on Christmas vacation early.

Santa says, "I can't believe you're back at work so soon after the fiasco. Don't get me wrong, you did the right thing, calling off the wedding." Santa's fairly understanding. He's one of my brothers' friends, Mammoth, in the local MC. Apparently, he and my brothers had talked about the marriage not seeming like a good thing.

Was it obvious to everyone except me?

Santa freezes, then leans to look past me, and raises a white-gloved hand. "Hey, didn't expect to see you here."

I turn, curious who showed up. The weakness in my knees, the fluttering in my chest, and the exhilaration that's zinging through my insides faster than Santa can circle the globe on Christmas Eve tell me exactly how I feel about my stepbrothers.

Knight, Axel, and Nova walk toward us on the red carpet laid over the fake snow. The lady with the kid and baby is smiling. Is this who she was holding a place for? Shit.

"Hey guys, do you need something?" I stammer.

Knight winks at me. Yes, I need that too. No, I can't think about that here.

"I'm at work. So seriously, did something come up?" I almost sound normal.

Axel snickers.

I try to step to the side to signal to the woman, but Nova grabs my arm. "Hold on. It's our turn."

"Your turn for what?"

"To make a wish." He points at Santa.

"This is for kids."

Nova leans to the side. "Santa, do you discriminate by age? You know you can't get away with that anymore."

Santa stays in character and does the deep belly laugh. He pats his leg. "Step right up. Tell me your deepest, darkest wish."

Oh, shit.

Nova says, "If you don't want us to sit on his lap and reveal our wishes, you can promise us another visit." He leans closer and lowers his voice. "I'll do better this time."

Better? He may not have fucked me the way he wanted to, but after he nutted all over me, he got me off with his hand. Being covered in the musky scent of his release intensified my orgasm to the point he had to carry me off the counter and hold me until I drifted back.

That's when I panicked and insisted they take me home. His strong arms holding me against his thick chest. His lips trailing little kisses in my hair. And the little murmuring when I swear he said, "I love you."

It all felt too good. And here they are making me want them more than ever. I'd planned on proving that sex was no big deal. I've never been more wrong. But I'm too afraid to say how much I want them.

"So be it." Nova smirks then lets go of my arm. He sits on Santa's lap while Knight and Axel stand on either side. The cameraman snaps a photo. It is fucking adorable. I'll give them that.

Santa takes it all in stride and gives the same line he's said a hundred times tonight. "What's your wish?"

My heart is caught in my throat.

I turn to Liz, "You can go. I've got—"

Knight's voice cuts me off. "We wish for a woman who'd be willing to share the three of us."

Axel says, "Who can handle our sometimes inappropriate humor."

Nova adds, "Who makes us as happy as we plan on making her."

I make Nova happy? And he plans on making me happy? He was my main partner in the 'no commitment' arena.

Santa says, "This will be a fun delivery. She can sit on my lap while Rudolph pulls my sleigh."

Knight objects, "Oh no, Santa. If she's sitting on a lap, it's going to be one of ours."

"All right. So what do you want her to look like?"

The guys talk over each other asking for light skin, long brown, straight hair, a wide smile that shows off her pretty teeth, but not in a weird way, a perky little nose, long legs...

Santa winks at me as I worry my lower lip. "Would you be happy if she was named Wendy?"

The guys laugh, but a public admission that they want me is scary.

Liz hasn't left yet. I'm sure nothing could compare to this freak show. She steps closer to me. "I know you're hesitant to commit right now but recognize an opportunity when it presents itself. Why not try this thing with your brothers? Hell, if you won't, I'm close enough to that description. I could let them call me Wendy."

She's joking, but the jealousy that flares through me makes it clear how I feel. Again. Am I going to keep denying all of the signs that things are good with my brothers?

"That's what I thought," she continues. "Instead of me leaving, you need to."

"I told you I'd take this shift."

"It's okay. I was just going to watch Hallmark Christmas movies and search online for new sparkly derby shorts. I can do it a different day."

Ten

Knight

Wendy agrees to meet us at the house. I'm tossing dirty laundry into the washing machine while Axel cleans the bathroom and Nova tackles the kitchen. We want to make a good impression when she gets here.

Santa, aka Mammoth, let us know that Wendy was taking a shift unexpectedly today and we rushed to meet her, not thinking ahead to what would happen if she accepted our offer to come back to our house.

She's so cautious right now, insisted on driving herself. She wants a way out. I can't falter for being hesitant about getting trapped. She's been trapped for way too long.

The doorbell ringing is a straight shot to my heart. How can we make so much mess?

"I wasn't sure if she was going to show," Axel says, "I thought she might've agreed just to get rid of us."

We help her with her coat and sit casually around the living room. It's anything but casual. We had to promise each other not to fight to sit next to her. Give her space. She chooses a spot on the couch.

She must have gone home and changed because she's not wearing the Santa's helper costume from the mall. The red and white striped stockings had me wanting to lick her like a piece of candy. That hasn't changed.

She switched to pink sweats and a T-shirt. She looks comfortable. That's how she should be. In fact, it makes the moment homey. Perfect.

"Did you bring a bag?" I ask, "You know, in case you decide to stay for the night."

"*Mi cama es su cama*." Nova grins.

"It's *mi casa es su casa*, amigo," Axel corrects.

"I meant what I said. Cama's bed in Spanish. You've got a place to sleep, or whatever. I'd like another chance to prove myself."

She lowers her face and tucks her hair behind her ear. "I'm sure you will. We can learn together."

This opens the conversation for what I've been wondering, and also a chance to razz Nova. "I'm happy to play the role of teacher. First of all, Nova, you're supposed to come *after* you put your dick in her."

"Fuck off, Knight. How about we start with a lesson about not judging each other? Tell us what you want to learn, Wendy," Nova gives me an understanding smile.

"Dad didn't let me date, so I've only stolen a few kisses. Then the heathen, because I refuse to say *his* name, first expressed an interest in me on my seventeenth birthday. At first, it was a badge of honor to have an older guy want me. I thought I was special. So naive. Now I know it's all a farce. I'm not special. I was a contract. So, basically, I need to learn everything."

"Whoa." I jump up, walk over to her, and drop to my knees. I take her hands from where she shoved them between her thighs. I hold them gently. "You are special. He's just a fucking idiot. And our Dad, he's power hungry. He always has been. It's why the three of us started our own accounting firm. We didn't want our legacy, if we even have one, to be tied to him. We wanted it to be something *we* made."

Axel cuts in. "Sorry we didn't think about you, sis, that he would leverage you like this."

I tread lightly, "Believe it or not, something seemed off and I was going to object to your wedding in that 'speak now or forever hold your peace' moment. But you beat me to it. You didn't need a hero." I take a breath. "I hope you want one, though."

"A hero... You were going to object?"

Axel says, "You wouldn't have done that. You're bullshitting."

Nova rubs his hands over his face. This is bound to dredge up discomfort.

"Check the inside pocket of my tux jacket."

"What's in it?" Wendy asks.

I lead her to my closet and point to the tux.

She side-eyes me then reaches inside. Retrieving the two pieces of paper, she holds them side by side and reads the fortune: *Claim your destiny with your heart, and the important things will fall into place.*

Axel takes the papers from her hand. "You had that at the wedding. Dad ripped it trying to get it from you."

"Yeah."

"You were going to object? And Dad knew?" Wendy says softly.

"Dad saw the fortune but had no idea what I planned on doing. I was going to object to protect you."

Nova says, "But she went with the runaway bride option, no hero needed." His voice cracks as he steps away from the closet. "I didn't realize Dad would stoop that low."

Damn him for killing the mood. Wendy tucks the fortune back into the pocket.

I say, "We could help you. We'll take care of you if you'll let us. We're a package deal. And if one of us turns into a jerk and tries to do some power play shit with you, the other two promise to kick his ass. Right, guys?"

Axel nods more enthusiastically than Nova. I add, "We'll set up a trust fund for you if that would make you feel better. Whether or not you are ready to commit to us. Just a gift to our sister. No strings attached."

"Please don't go setting up any trust funds. I'm applying for jobs and want to prove that I can take care of myself. Just like you did. I've been reading interview skills on the internet and doing practice questions out loud in front of the mirror."

"Hold on, I see an opportunity," I say. "We've conducted a lot of interviews. We could help you practice. In fact," I stand up and head to the kitchen to grab my keys. "We could go to the office and role play."

"I love role play." She practically leaps from the couch. In seconds we're all piling onto our bikes. I make sure she's on the back of mine.

At the office, she sits in the lobby instead of heading down the hallway with us. "Come on. Let's do the interview."

"The secretary has to call me back." She picks up a magazine, crosses her legs, and ignores us.

"Axel, you take the desk. Nova, you'll be with me and we'll do a panel-style interview. Axel, once you finish your role as secretary, join us."

We take our spots in the office that has minimalist decor, a neutral place for conducting interviews, away from our personal offices. Rather than sitting at the desk, I grab pens and paper then lead Nova to the oak table. It's sturdy enough to support us climbing on top of it.

"Set her chair out there." I motion a few feet from the desk. It will give me room to kneel in front of her.

Axel knocks on the door, then pops his head in. "Mr. Russell and Mr. Russell, are you ready for the interview?"

"Yeah, bring her in." Rather than looking up from the paper in front of me, I lift my hand and wave a couple of fingers. "Come on in..." I pretend to be looking for her name. "Ms. Cooper."

"Thank you, sir."

"Have a seat," Nova says.

Axel continues as secretary, taking pretend notes. We go through a few formalities and her poise impresses me. But we're not really here to practice. Time to segue to the fun part of the interview.

"Ms. Cooper, how would you rate your multitasking skills?"

"I like to think that I'm good at multitasking. I can handle multiple things in motion at one time, but I've read numerous studies that say it's more efficient to focus on a single task. But I'm versatile. I'll do whatever the job dictates." The lightness in her voice indicates she knows I'm up to something.

"Interesting. How about this?" I walk around the desk and drop to my knees in front of her. "May I?" My hands hover above her thighs.

"Of course, sir. It's your office. Whatever you want. I want to ace this interview."

"Okay. Let's test your multitasking skills. Nova, my partner, is going to continue asking you questions while I feast on your pussy. Let's see if you can truly do two things at once."

She allows me to slip her sweats and panties off. I'd rather ditch the role play, but it seems to help her relax. My erection is about to bust my jeans open.

I spread her legs wider, but when the edges of the chair prevent me from splaying her open, I reach around and pull her ass forward. It's like pulling the buffet table to my mouth. I want to dive in with full gluttony.

With mock professionalism, I kiss my way up her thighs and over her pussy before sliding my tongue between her sweet lips. Her swollen nub grows harder as her breaths become more erratic. Her answers to Nova's questions take increasing time and are less coherent.

There's nothing I love more than making her lose control, except for doing it with my dick.

When she cries out, I slow my pace, easing her through the climax. Her head is tipped back, her hands tangled in my hair, and her mouth open. I sit back on my heels. I'm not ready to return to my seat, so I hang out in heaven between her legs.

Continuing the interview, I give her a minute then assess the situation. "Screw the studies. You did a great job putting your primary focus on having an orgasm. Your secondary focus shifted to tangling your fingers in my hair. I'm giving that a thumbs up. Let's get Nova's report."

Her smile takes my focus away from my cock. My heart is full. I want to make this woman happy for the rest of my life.

"The more she focused on orgasming, the more trouble she had answering questions. But that's only one test. I'd like to try another situation if you don't mind. And if Axel can stop taking notes, I think we should all participate."

Axel slaps the pen and notebook on the table. "Tell me what we need to do."

"Okay, Ms. Cooper, I'd like you to strip naked, then lie down on this table. Would you be comfortable with that?"

"I think I'll be comfortable with anything you ask me to do."

"That's a very teamwork-friendly answer. We like that."

"What kind of multitasking do you want to test this time?"

"I'm going to fuck you and you're going to either have your hand or your mouth on their cocks. Do you think you can focus on all three tasks at once?"

Way to go, Nova.

The façade of role play cracks briefly with her laughter. "I think I'm perfectly suited for this."

The scent of her sex already fills the small room. My cock throbs and springs free when I strip my clothes. I've never been naked like this with my brothers, the key factor being the naked woman climbing back onto the table.

I tip her face to the side and tap my cock on her mouth. She scoots toward the edge to reach it easier. Poor Axel will have to go for her hand. Although watching her bright pink manicured nails wrap around his shaft, he's not losing much.

There's still no conversation about birth control. Everyone has to be thinking about it. Nova positions himself in Wendy's curls. He gets his footing stabilized. Pre-cum drips out. He could be getting her pregnant right now.

Wendy's tongue roams the tip of my cock but all I can think is that Nova needs to hurry.

He drags a thumb over his pre-cum, rubbing it into her glistening curls.

"Fuck."

His eyes meet mine and I realize I said that out loud.

His evil grin gives way to him saying, "I'm putting this inside of her to make sure she's ready."

Lowering my eyes, my cock twitches. Nova catches another drip of pre-cum from his tip then slides it into her cunt. He's teasing me, the little shit.

She shudders under his touch for what seems like an eternity before he fists his shaft and pushes his strained head into her wet lips.

"Remember how much cum I had for you last time?"

She pulls away from my cock and offers a breathy, "It was everywhere."

"It's all going inside this time. I'm going to fill you up." Nova's eyes roll back as he slides inside of Wendy for the first time. I figure we don't have long. He grips her thighs, then repositions, lifting her legs so that her feet are at his shoulders.

He wraps his arms around her legs, holding her into him as he thrusts. Grunts and groans rumble from him.

Wendy licks my tip until Nova sets his rhythm. She opens her mouth, taking me in while stroking me with her tongue. Her beautiful red plump lips seal on my shaft, locking in my pleasure. She's sucking me into oblivion. She certainly doesn't need any lessons on cock sucking.

I fist her hair, guiding her head carefully so that she doesn't have to move much while getting railed. As I work my hips, I'm getting close, but hold my release back. I shift my attention between watching Nova fuck a woman for the first time, Wendy's hand driving Axel crazy, and her mouth stretched around me.

We make a great team. I could exist here forever. We could rotate around this desk, each taking turns pleasing her.

On this rotation, her moans vibrate my shaft, building my orgasm to heights I haven't been to before. Then Nova growls out his release. Good thing nobody's in the building. They could have heard it on every single floor.

He promised to fill her, and he did. I watch between her legs as his seed spills out. The sound of bodies, slapping with wetness, sends me dangerously close to the edge. I thrust forward and fill her mouth with my release.

She gags and gasps for air so I fist my cock, keeping the tip in her pretty lips. Like a trouper, she regroups, seals her lips on my shaft, and sucks for dear life. When I can breathe again, I say, "Such a good girl."

She smiles up at me with my cock still in her mouth. At least I think it's a smile, but a white flash interrupts our tender moment. Axel's pumping cum across her tits, even hit me. Fuck. That's messed up.

But while she keeps pumping Axel's shaft, she keeps her lips on me.

Fuck, what's happening. My balls grow heavy, tighten, and blow another load down her throat. Damn. I've never had a double release before.

There's no way I can let her go.

Eleven

Wendy

Braiding ribbons into my hair, I get ready for the special Christmas fundraiser roller derby bout.

My legs are weak after an evening with my brothers, but if that had been a real interview, it would be safe to say I'd get hired. The question is if I want to be hired...as their girlfriend. Is that what I'd be? Or just fuck toy?

I keep trying to tell myself that's all I want—Brothers with benefits. Fantasy Wendy keeps interrupting to insist that I commit.

My video messaging app rings. It's Dad. I quickly get to the end of my braid and tie a bow around the end. I forgot that we'd connected on here before.

Deciding to stand up for myself has been a big move for me, and if I'm going to do that, I might as well talk to Dad now. If we can repair our relationship, great. If he can't see that what he did is wrong, I'll get my frustrations out during the bout.

"Hi, Dad," I say.

"Wendy." He nods.

I take a deep breath. Don't let it get to me that he's impersonal. He's never been personable. "I only have a few minutes. I have a roller derby bout, but I want to talk to you."

"Since you mentioned roller derby, are you still doing that?"

Duh. "Yes, it's very important to me, Dad. We do charity work, plus it's great exercise."

"It's not appropriate for a woman to go out and act like that."

"My teammates disagree." It's a bold move for me to say that, but I feel supported now that my brothers are on my side. "It's one of the many roles I play in this world. If you want to judge me, then we can end the call right now." I reach for the End Call button.

"Wait, don't hang up. Your mother and I have talked and she asked me to make amends with you."

"Okay." I'm cautious since the call got off to a bad start.

"This is me officially saying that I can see how you would be unhappy about the marriage. You aren't old enough to understand how difficult the business world is and the importance of family legacies. That you wouldn't want to be *used*. That's your mother's word. I could have been clearer with you at the outset about why my friend was interested in you."

I take a second. Does he believe this is an apology? "Used...yes. And worse, traded, treated like property..."

"It doesn't sound great when you put it like that, but when you're older you'll understand love is overrated. But with skilled negotiating on my part, the partnership talks are continuing. He'd still prefer that you be involved, but if you refuse, he will still consider partnering with our company. He sees the value in what I've built even if you don't."

"Dad, this isn't an apology. You tried to sell my virginity?"

"What on earth are you talking about, Wendy? How would I know if you're a virgin?"

Shit. This is embarrassing. "Oops, that one's on me. I drew a conclusion."

"Did he try..." My father's voice wavers with a shred of decency.

"No. Never." Oh boy, that makes the auction thing a ridiculous choice. Good thing we don't have to discuss that.

"Good. I've built myself up from nothing and I don't want you to have to do the same."

The sad truth is that as angry as I am with my dad, I still love him. I know that he means well. He'll have to earn his spot in my life though.

"Maybe I don't mind doing the same. I need to learn who I am, and it's not a contract bride. I'm a human. I'm your daughter. I need time to get to know myself with or without you."

"I can agree to those terms."

Those terms? I stick that irritation in the front of my brain where I can pluck it out to use during the bout. But guilt pangs inside of me for not telling him the full story. I try to speak on his terms.

"We have to make risk assessments, right, Dad? I've listened. I've learned things. Just give me a chance to sort myself out."

He smiles when I say risk assessment.

"That's what your mother said. I have to give you time. I'll do it, but I can't guarantee which position I'll have open for you whenever you decide to come back."

"Dad, I need you to be my father, not my employer. I need someone I can turn to when I have questions about life, when I need support, when I feel like everyone turns against me."

"That's hard for me. I'm not the emotional type."

"Can you just be there to listen? You listened to mom and you're on the phone with me, that's a start."

He smiles. "I suppose I can commit to listening. I do love you, Wendy."

"I know you do, in your own way, but not working together will be the best way to nurture that."

Nikki rolls into the locker room. "Five-minute call."

"Sorry, Dad. I've got to go. We can talk later."

"I'll have my people call you and set up a time."

"No, Dad, we're not going to have our people talk. We're going to do it." For the first time, my dad might truly respect that I'm not his property.

How damaging will my secret relationship be if he finds out?

Twelve

Axel

We showed up for Wendy's roller derby bout, but in the interest of making it less obvious, we invited the whole MC. It was pretty easy to convince the rest of the gang to come watch girls in spandex get rough and sweaty with each other.

"Our sister's off-limits," I remind my brothers. Not my birth brothers, my found family of brothers in the MC. "She's number twenty-three, Roll Play."

It's hard enough for me to share her with my brothers. I want her to myself.

Catcalls and general rowdiness erupt as the derby girls take the track. They joke about my claim, but I know they heard me.

I get lost in thought. Her derby name...Roll Play. She likes pretending. Is that because she's been escaping the reality of her world, even if just subconsciously knowing she wasn't loved for herself? It hurts. How the hell does she deal with it?

Is there similarity to how I get caught in my head, missing things that are right in front of me?

I want to ride home and tell Dad to apologize for everything he ever said that made her think she wasn't enough, and to give her job back. But mostly, I want to take Wendy in my arms and hold her, protect her from the world.

Could I do that with Knight and Nova by my side? We could make sure she's safe to be herself. Nobody fucking judging her or telling her what to do, and with the extended family of the rest of the MC, she'd never be at risk.

Watching her skate and crash into other women, the intensity on her face is insane. It's a little reminiscent of when she was younger and would try to get a toy that we were keeping from her. She still has an innocence about her, but she's jaded.

Rightly so. I fucking hate everyone who's done that to her. I can't think about it.

My eyes are glued to my sweet princess, Roll Play, as a member of the other team makes an illegal move and shoves her out of bounds. My girl is smart. She knows how to fall. I hate that she's had to learn that.

Shit. I'm all messed up. She chooses to learn that so she can skate safely. She doesn't need me there to catch her, to protect my little sister.

I wish I could get a better read on her. It terrifies me that our relationship doesn't feel superficial to me, yet I'm not sure how she sees it. After the wedding fiasco, we might never be able to break down her walls and convince her that love can be different.

Sitting in the bleachers with Nova and Knight, knowing that they feel the same for her as I do, and the rest of our club surrounding us, I realize that what works about this is that we are willing to share her.

That's what works in our club. We share responsibility for each other. In that light, it's fine to want Knight and Nova to be part of the relationship. We'll share responsibility for Wendy.

We have a big mission ahead of us—convince her that she's special. I hated her saying she wasn't special the other night. The truth is that my brothers and I might not be worthy of her.

But she may never be ready to go public with us. She might have her fun then pick guys her own age. A headache sets in. I wouldn't be able to handle her dating another guy. I scan the bleachers, my eyes landing on a guy her age, and I automatically want to strangle him.

The crowd goes wild as the final whistle blows. I stand and cheer. Our girl's team won. Time to celebrate by doing some more role play with Roll Play.

Thirteen

Wendy

The ends of my braids blow backward below my helmet as we fly down the road. I'd gotten a ride with Beatrix to the derby arena, so no problem figuring out what to do with my car when my brothers offered to take me home.

The ride to my brothers' house gives me time to sort my thoughts. Hearing them and many other members of their MC cheering us on, I realized how much they support me. How much each member of the MC supports all of the other members. They're more of a family than we had at home.

Our parents don't approve of the guys being in an MC any more than they approve of me doing roller derby. None of us kids grew up the way our parents wanted us to. That's not my fault, or my brothers'. We are who we are.

It's a turning point for me to realize I'm not wrong. I can choose my path. And right now, the path I'd like to explore is with my brothers. But that's all it is—an exploration.

We turn into the Cherry Ridge foothills, winding our way to their isolated home. Good thing they pay someone to keep their road plowed, the snow is starting to stick. The bumps and bruises that plague me after every bout seem less with my new sense of freedom.

Pulling up to their house, Axel lowers the kickstand, then hops off. I start to dismount but he sets his hand on my shoulder. "Hang on."

He helps remove my helmet. "I've had a goddamn boner watching you sweat and grind with all those women. I need you, Wendy."

"I need you too." Being consumed by a physical need for someone is new for me. And we get along so well otherwise. In our little bubble. We're a long way from exposing ourselves. Clouds move in front of the full moon, protecting our space with darkness.

"I want to fuck you out here where it's wild and raw under the night sky. Nothing between us and the world. You good with that, Roll Play?"

The play on words of my derby name rings so true with my guys. "Which role should I take now?"

"Be mine."

That feels too intimate. I don't want them to think I'm committing to more than I'm ready for. "Axel—"

He puts a finger on my lips. "Shhh, just let me have you."

My heart says yes, but my head is still a mess. Is silence my way of chickening out, not being clear that I'm one hundred percent ready to commit physically but struggling with the rest? Or is my surrender enough?

He grabs the ribbon holding one of my braids, pulling a single end slowly as he watches it untie. Then he fishes the other braid from behind my shoulder, pulls it forward, and removes that ribbon. He hands one to each of our brothers.

"Get her naked and on my lap, then tie her hands behind her back."

There's a pause while they visually check in with me. I nod, my breath coming with audible heaviness. They strip my lower half bare. I should be cold in the winter night air, but they're close and my body's on fire.

Axel tosses his clothes aside and sits on his bike, his erection standing tall in front of his ripped abs. Our brothers lift me onto his lap and carefully position my feet so they don't touch anything hot. I question if I'm hotter than anything on this bike.

Nova and Knight work together to bind my hands. The position thrusts my breasts shamelessly at Axel. My sex is open for him. His cock stands ready for me. Correction to my earlier thought. Now, I've never felt so free.

The dark sky with twinkling stars. The light breeze that can't quite cool me off. And the freedom surrendering to my brothers. This is how I want to live.

Axel's hands wrap around my waist and he adjusts his hips to notch his cock at my entrance. I slide down. My body stretches around him. I stare at him, wondering how I can feel this good.

The other two brothers stay close, making sure I'm safe since I can't balance myself, but also making sure they're involved.

"You look so fucking good riding him," Knight says.

"If you were doing this to anyone but my brother, I'd have to beat the shit out of someone," Nova says. "You fucking make my cock eternally hard."

Axel kisses my neck, and massages my breasts. Knight and Nova are intimate with me from either side, but I can't touch any of them. All I can do is accept what they offer, and give in to every thrust of Axel's shaft as he makes me whole.

And possibly more than whole if our unprotected sex has consequences. Am I finally ready to admit that Fantasy Wendy was right?

It's a dangerous thought, made even worse by how quickly I come and how quickly I pull his release from him. I'm limp in his embrace. I'm completely at their mercy. I've surrendered and I'm happy.

Physically we're perfect together. But a relationship has to be more than a physical connection. We need to be friends too. And we are. We have to respect our differences. And we do. But I thought that with he-who-won't-be-named. It was too perfect, just like this. Well, not *just* like this.

Axel whispers. "I love you, Wendy."

Knight joins him, "Damn, I love you, Wendy."

Nova looks away. His chest expands and releases. He faces me, and his words are intentional. "I love you, Wendy."

It all happens so fast, I can't stop them before they all say it. Anxiety wells inside of me. How can they know they love me? What even is love? And why did Nova have to say it? Is his declaration proof that we're moving too fast like he's always done?

The intimacy comes crashing down. The bright light of the full moon shines like a glaring spotlight in my eyes, exposing me, blinding me. I'm uncomfortable. I turn my face away, unable to defend myself.

Only one other man than my father has said he loved me. He didn't love *me*, no matter how good it felt to hear his words.

"Untie me."

"Hey, hey. Slow down." Axel grips me with both hands.

I twist my shoulders. "Untie me now."

"We will. Calm down."

Knight takes control. His hand around my wrist is met with sudden freedom as the ribbon falls free. "What's wrong?"

"This isn't love. This is lust and sex and... Just let me go."

Nova looks sick as he turns, walking away from us.

Axel says, "I thought we were—"

"You can't say love. That's not what this is."

The hurt in their expressions tells me I might be wrong.

Axel wraps an arm around my shoulder as Knight helps me get my clothes on. No one's worried about the cum dripping down my leg. No one needs to be. The worst problem is what's left inside of me and what they put inside of me previously.

I am just a foolish girl. My dad was right. I'm too screwed up to trust that people can love me.

Fourteen

Nova

I knew better than to say those three little fucking words. Why couldn't I keep my damn mouth shut?

Anger flows through my veins. Why did I storm away from them? My bike was right there. My hands itch to grab the handlebars, rev the throttle, and put miles between us.

Wendy's going to break my heart.

Reaching in my pocket, freedom is offered by the small metal key. I pull it out, ready to ride. Ready to be anywhere but here. Ready to...

I turn toward my bike and see Wendy. I see her pain. Something happens inside my chest. She's as hurt as I am. We're all pawns in someone else's game.

I step toward my bike. Toward freedom. Just get on. That's all I have to do to escape this shitshow. She made it clear she doesn't want to go public with our relationship. We're just fun to her. Even her goddamn roller derby name proves it. She just plays roles, pretends, and has her fun and leaves.

My chest tightens. I press my hand into my shirt, but the pain doesn't let up. Fuck! Am I having a heart attack?

Two more steps to my bike, and my chest hurts worse with each one. I won't be a coward. I'm man enough to say goodbye. I angle my head.

Her eyes meet mine. She's so young. So talented. I don't deserve someone like her. The three of us ganged up on her, not giving her time to breathe after one of the hardest decisions of her life—standing up to Father.

Wendy makes me a better person. I take a lesson from her and face my fear.

"Fuck!" So many emotions storm inside of me, I unintentionally scream to vent. All eyes land on me.

The key falls from my fingers, nestling itself deep in my pocket.

Knight and Axel will be pissed. They don't matter. The foolish belief that we could all take care of Wendy is our fault. Not hers. When it's over it's over, I've certainly become an expert on that. She doesn't want us and we need to accept it like grown men.

Wendy slips a sock on and ties her shoe.

I nod toward the house. "Give me a minute with Wendy."

When we're alone, I say, "You've been clear with us from the start, we just didn't want to see the writing on the wall." Motioning to my bike, I continue, "Hop on, I'll take you home."

Fifteen

Wendy

A pain in my hip wakes me from the minute of sleep I managed for the night. I roll onto my back and rub the sore spot. I remember all too clearly bouncing that hip off the derby track last night. I rotate my leg to get some blood flowing and ease the pain a little.

If only I could mend my heart so easily. It hurts worse than any other body part. I lift my pajama top, sure there will be a bruise on my chest. There's not.

A sleepless night has turned into a day I don't want to face, and a decision I don't know how to make.

There was so much hurt in Nova's eyes when he gave me the option to go home. I flop an arm over my eyes.

Why did I have to freak out the second he said he loves me? Can I blame it on the rebound?

I can't be the woman three men, who happen to be my brothers, need. I'm just an eighteen-year-old, trying not to get married as part of a business deal.

They were there to catch me when I fell, and look how I repay them.

My heart pumps a different emotion with each beat. One beat I'm angry with them for being older and knowing better. They shouldn't have put me in this position.

Then it beats sympathy for them. They offered and I accepted. I can't blame them.

Then it beats sadness that there's so much strife in my family right now. Another beat, resentment for the way my father treated me. Another beat, disbelief that my mother would allow my father to do that. She may be my stepmom, but she's the only mom I remember.

The next beat is mushy and wiggly. It doesn't make sense. It's an emotion I haven't dealt with before. It begs me to trust it, but how do I trust the unknown?

I won't be fooled. This is Fantasy Wendy. She's wild and carefree. She's also imaginary. She doesn't have to live with consequences.

I have to end this. I have to find my worth, no matter how good it feels to be with my brothers. No matter that my favorite role is to be theirs. I need to play the role of Wendy first and figure out who she is.

The video app on my phone buzzes. It's Dad. I'm not up for a video chat. I showered thoroughly last night, trying to convince myself that I had to wash myself clean. Free from my brothers, free from everything except me. No smeared makeup, no sweat, just me.

Dad won't be happy knowing that I've slept in until... I look at the clock on my phone. It's after nine.

I sit up and clear my throat before accepting the call with audio only.

"Hey Dad, can't put you on video right now." I stick with the truth.

"That's not exactly what I wanted to hear. Are you with your brothers? Are you having sex with them? Don't answer that. I heard about what happened at the sex club."

I'm too stunned to say anything. He doesn't need me to.

"The humiliation that you're bringing to this family is unequaled. Do you think you're one of those people who's going to find fame and celebrity by leaking a sex tape? Do you think that because we have money, you can do anything you want? I absolutely will not have that in my family. You can watch your email for an official notification from the lawyer that my will has been rewritten and you are no longer in it. And your mother is in full agreement."

The call goes dead, on par with my soul.

A few seconds pass before my mother's strained voice adds, "I'm in full agreement with your father. This is unacceptable behavior."

Did I get what I asked for? I get to figure out who I am with no access to my family's fortune. I resist opening my bank app to see if he closed my account. I don't think he'd want me to live on the streets, but I'm not ready to be sure.

My parents continue to drive their point home and I half-heartedly listen.

I'm not ready to face the world so utterly on my own. A million ideas run through my mind of how I can minimize my lifestyle.

I flip to my email to see if any of the companies have responded to my job applications. Not yet. I'll send more applications today. It's time to take care of myself.

Sixteen

Wendy

I text Nikki to catch her up on things and she offers to come over, but I need to get my big girl activities done before I chicken out.

I text back: *Thanks. I may take you up on it later*

Nikki: *Are you sure? I'm grabbing my keys*

Me: *No, I need to handle this*

She sends a GIF of a car fishtailing as it speeds around a corner.

Me: *I promise I'll be in touch later today*

I pull up the sibling chat. *Can we meet?*

I swear the message hasn't even had time to send when all three guys respond.

Nova asks: *Where*

Knight: *When*

Axel: *yes*

We agree to meet at their office because I need to be somewhere that I can try not to fall apart. I need to be somewhere to remind myself of professionalism and responsibility. And they're already there, so that makes it easy.

The secretary tells me they're wrapping up a meeting and directs me to an empty conference room. The interior blinds are closed so no one can see in. I take a seat.

That wiggly, squishy, evasive feeling hasn't left my chest. Sitting alone, I try to figure it out. It reminds me of snuggling on my grandfather's lap while he told stories of his childhood. Of hanging out with my best friends in high school. Of getting the boss's approval of my graphic designs. Of getting accepted onto the roller derby team.

All good feelings. All supportive. All about belonging. The emotions grow stronger and stronger as each realization hits me. Oh crap. I think this might be love. Everything starts clicking into place.

Fine time for the revelation. Or is Fantasy Wendy getting more savvy, and tricking me since I'm a bit desperate?

For now, stick to my mission... I owe my brothers a gigantic apology. At the very least, I need their friendship.

Cindy pops her head in. I'm so self-absorbed, I forgot she'd be here since she works for my brothers. She was in the auction too, also won by her stepbrothers. I guess she hasn't quit her job to live a fantasy life with them.

"What's going on? Is everything okay with your brothers?"

"I can't blame them." It's hard to finish my thought.

"What happened?" She looks worried.

"Is it terrible to have sex with our stepbrothers?"

She rolls her eyes. "I took two wrong turns driving here. I might not be the best person to ask for advice." She sits next to me and takes my hand. "Are you concerned about the act of sex, or is your heart the question?"

"Have you told your parents yet?" Living in a bubble versus living openly makes a big difference.

"No."

"My dad was upset that I walked out of my wedding, which he'd carefully crafted as a business deal. And when he found out I hooked up with my stepbrothers..." I flop my hands as if presenting myself. "Who wants tarnished goods? He was so mad he wrote me out of the will and said I better hang up my roller skates and get a real job."

"There are so many things wrong with that. You're far from tarnished. You only do roller derby for fun. And who—"

Knight, Axel, and Nova file into the room looking insanely stern. Cindy and I wish each other well and she leaves.

"We're glad you're ready to see us." Nova rushes to my side.

"I'm so sorry for the way I treated all of you."

"You didn't do anything wrong," Axel says.

"I did, but I've come to my senses, and I have to be completely honest with you so you don't find out otherwise. Dad wrote me out of his will. And I realize I said I wanted to figure life out on my own, but family was my safety net."

Saying it out loud, I understand why my brothers separated themselves from my dad's empire. They didn't want to be controlled like this.

"That's what family is supposed to be. In our case, it's money. In other families, it's warmth, compassion, and support."

"And now I have none of that."

"You do, you have all of it with us." Knight waves me off when I open my mouth to speak. "We've been talking this morning. There's something we need to know. If we weren't your brothers, would you have been open to a relationship?"

I'm stymied by his question. Did I have trouble with the timing, the sibling thing, the number of guys, the speed I fell for them? "It's so hard to say."

"You were auctioning yourself. Anyone could have bought you. If you'd hit it off with strangers, would you have committed to them?"

"I can't answer that question."

"Why?"

"Because I just figured it out. I know who I am. I am a woman who's admired the way you stood up to my dad. Without him, you built your business from the ground up. You were a role model for me to escape my wedding. And even when I was clinging to him for understanding, you clung to me. You found your own supportive family in your motorcycle club. I want to be a part of that. I want to not just have one man, but three men who love me."

It's their turn to be shocked.

"I don't just want to role play sex games. I know which role I want. I want to be your..." I stop Fantasy Wendy just in time. She jumped in and was about to say 'wife'.

Knight kneels and takes my hands. I love it when he does that.

"You don't have to say anything you're not ready for. You've been through a lot. And I know I can speak for these fuckers when I say, you've just made us the happiest men in the world."

We end up in a hug that I'm finally happy I can fully enjoy. Fantasy Wendy joins us. Maybe Real-World Wendy and Fantasy Wendy aren't all that different.

"One more thing. I'm ready to commit to the three of you, but I have one important requirement." I pause.

Knight says, "Hit us with it. I'm sure it will be fine."

"We have to tell our parents." I'm not sure how I expect my brothers to react, but Knight's smirk isn't it.

Seventeen

Nova

Axel and I join Knight kneeling on the floor and I spin Wendy's chair so she faces me.

"Consider it done."

Wendy bites her lower lip and catches Knight and Axel nodding at me. Before she can ask what's up I go for it.

"We want you to understand how committed we are to you, even if it means giving you more space than we want." I reach into my pocket and pull out a black box, opening it to display the diamond ring. "When the time is right, this ring is yours."

Her hands fly to her mouth and her first few attempts at words come out garbled. Knight rubs her back, helping her calm down.

"When did you buy this?"

"Knight had it before your wedding. And when this group thing happened, we took it to the jeweler to modify it to represent all of us."

It's beyond gorgeous. I suck in a breath to calm my threatening tears. "That's so sweet. But why would you do that?"

Axel says, "We knew we wanted to marry you."

Knight adds, "And wanted to knock you up. If you didn't notice, we didn't ask about birth control."

"So I'm not crazy for being careless," she asks.

"It's fine, as long as you're only with us," I say.

Knight explains, "I bought it before I ever had sex with you, even though you couldn't know that. I hoped that if you ever got worried about why we were with you, we could use it to show how far we'd fallen for you. We weren't just with you because you're the best sex any of us have ever had."

Axel quips. "Especially Nova."

I glare at him. No time for sibling bickering though.

Knight says, "Remember the fortune?"

She nods. "You might be as caught in fantasies if you think a fortune could tell you we were supposed to get married."

"Trust me. I've never paid attention to wisdom from a cookie. But, I got the fortune at your eighteenth birthday party. I had just broken the cookie open and was reading it when I overheard you accepting a marriage proposal."

"No way."

"Full honesty. That's what happened. I wasn't sure what to do, so I slipped it into my wallet. I'd denied my feelings for you, and the whole idea of marrying my sister seemed ridiculous until everything started falling into place."

I steal the show back from Knight. "We love you for who you are. We watched you defy Dad and join roller derby. We watched you choose your own career path in graphic arts instead of number crunching or market analysis or any of the other jobs Dad approves of. We watched you take control of your future when you realized he was using you to advance his business—"

"You mean *legacy*?" Wendy laughs.

"That too. Those are just the big things. You're strong. You've always known who you are. And if someday you choose to add *our wife* to that list, it'll be our honor."

"Seeing myself through your eyes, I don't feel nearly as screwed up." She extends her hand and we stare at it before I realize what she's doing. I fumble the box. Axel catches it. Knight grabs the ring and slides it on her finger.

"I'm more than ready to be your wife. And since I'm probably pregnant, the sooner we do this, the less explaining we'll have. So you're good with telling our parents?"

"We are," Knight says emphatically. "In fact, we had a long talk with Dad and Mom this morning. He called us, furious at what we'd done in the sex club and we told him to come say it to our face. So he did. We've been talking to them all morning."

Axel says. "He's not happy about it. Mom isn't quite as upset, but we convinced them to write you back into the will."

"What? They're here? And you convinced them?"

I take the seat beside Wendy. "Want me to call them in?"

Fortified by the presence of my brothers, and now fiancées, we sit around the table as they have the secretary get our parents. We're lined up on one side and they sit on the opposite side.

Knight insists on being the one to do this. "Mom. Dad. We appreciate you hearing us out this morning and rewriting Wendy into your will. Now we have one other bomb to drop."

"Really? Dictating how I conduct my affairs isn't enough? What more could you want?"

I consider saying that we want their blessing for our marriage, but we'll be fine without it.

"We're engaged."

Dad coughs and sputters and pushes away from the table. He stands and paces.

Mom forces a smile and says, "Engaged?"

I lift Wendy's hand to reveal the ring.

Mom's smile grows more genuine. "For real engaged?"

Knight says, "It's for real, the way Wendy deserves it. For love."

Eighteen

Axel

Mom and Dad are at our house for Christmas Day. It's the first time they've come over since our big reveal last week, which was promptly followed by Wendy moving in.

Dad does his best to remain cordial. He's truly trying to accept our relationship. Mom's openly good with our choice now that she understands we're committed to one another. She didn't know about the business deal marriage and had it out with Dad. She keeps him on a tight leash now.

But Wendy had a stroke of insight that we have to get our parents up to speed on everything. It won't be long before people talk about how quickly we're getting married, and shortly after that, they'll do the math on when the baby's due.

Wendy reasoned that we tell our parents about the baby now, so they feel included. That allows them to address it with friends and family however they wish.

Christmas dinner wraps up. The gift exchange is over. Dad's gift was the nicest of all. He stepped out of the business deal with the man who wanted to marry Wendy. It was a huge contract, so we appreciate the consequences of not going through with it. One of the nicest gestures he's ever made.

And now Dad's getting grumbly about heading home to watch the football game. "Thanks for having us. We better get going."

"Before you do," I say, casting a glance at my brothers and sister. They all nod, so I continue. "We sincerely appreciate your support for our upcoming marriage. We know it's not easy. And we want to be as open with you as possible."

"I'm trying, son. But teaching an old dog new tricks has never been easy."

"He'll come around," Mom says.

"Speak for yourself, woman." He smiles at mom. "I just don't understand why the rush on the wedding. It's not like you have a contract deadline to meet." At least he's able to take himself down a notch.

But we do have a deadline. "That's what we want to talk to you about. Are you ready for this?"

Mom's face lights up. I'm pretty sure she caught on. Her eyes move to Wendy's belly. There's a chance it was a coincidence because Wendy's holding a present, but Mom's smart.

Dad says, "Am I ready? How am I supposed to know?"

Mom swats him. "Hurry, say yes."

"Why?"

"You really can't think of a reason they'd get married quickly?"

"To spite me?" Dad's actually confused.

Wendy extends the gift. "Maybe this will help."

Mom snatches the present, rips the paper off, throwing it at Dad, and stares at the picture Wendy designed, trying to use terms he loves. It says:

Project: Grandparents

Status: in negotiation

Deadline: September

"We're going to be grandparents. Isn't that exciting?" Mom squeals then puts her arm around Dad, who stares at the picture silently.

The rest of us stare at him.

"They're sharing their lives with us. Be grateful." Worry tinges Mom's comment.

Dad takes a breath and when he lifts his head, I swear his eyes are a little shiny. He recovers quickly. "Maybe I shouldn't have written you all back into the will. You're doing your best to give this old man a heart attack."

I think that was a joke. My eyes scan everyone else. No one's sure.

"Congratulations," he says, and we breathe a collective sigh of relief. He shakes my hand then Knight's and Nova's before turning to Wendy.

He wraps her in a hug. "If they don't take good care of you, let me know. I'm going to try to be a better father."

"Thanks, Dad. That won't be a problem. They treat me better than anyone else ever has."

Epilogue

Axel

Dad escorts Mom down the aisle. It was Wendy's choice to have it this way, just like her first wedding. Fear ripples through me at how close we were to losing her that day.

The wedding planner nudges my shoulder. "That's your cue."

I take a deep breath before moving my foot forward. It's not that I'm nervous or have cold feet like other grooms. It's the disbelief that I've learned how to be more myself through Wendy, my little sister, my love, and soon-to-be my wife.

Knight and Nova fall into step behind me, just as Wendy wanted it. The three of us make our way to the front. We drew our order out of a hat because we couldn't find any rational way to choose, and the aisle wasn't large enough for us to fit side by side. So, not only am I first, but as I take my place at the front of the church, my brothers flank me. I get to stand directly in front of Wendy.

Thankfully she doesn't have horrible morning sickness like her friend Cindy. That wedding day got messy.

The bridesmaids enter, pulling me back to the moment, and I'm surprised by my jealousy. They've seen Wendy today. They know how divine she looks in her wedding dress, which we were expressly forbidden from seeing.

I glance down the line of women: blue hair, a pinup girl, an arm in a sling. She has quite the assortment of friends.

The music shifts to *Somebody Loves You* by Betty Who.

I turn my attention to the back of the church where the bottom of a full white dress appears in the entryway. How big is her skirt?

Why did she stop? Worry races through my mind that she could be backing out, getting cold feet. It wouldn't matter that she's pregnant, she doesn't *have* to marry us. It's her choice.

I glance at Nova, who looks as if he's about to vomit. Maybe today won't be much cleaner than Cindy's wedding.

But as I'm watching my brother, his expression relaxes, and pure joy covers his face.

Returning my attention to the back, I understand. Wendy rounded the corner. She's more beautiful than ever.

She's the last of the women who were in this year's Christmas Cherry Auction to get married. There was less urgency with her since she's only pregnant with a single baby. Honestly, it was an ego blow. My brothers and I felt like we hadn't done our job correctly. But since she's not as pregnant as her friends, it was fair to let the other women go first.

As pregnant...No. Our girl is one hundred percent pregnant. If it's possible for me to smile any wider, I do, although I'm starting to wonder if I'm going to look like a fool in the wedding pictures.

The photographer has his camera pointed at Wendy, so I clench my jaw and work my lips to relax my mouth. It immediately pulls into a smile again. I can't contain how happy I am.

In her big poofy, lace-covered dress, Wendy looks like the princess she is. But she doesn't get one prince charming, she gets three.

A chuckle rolls through me as I notice ribbons braided through her trademark pigtails, tidy little bows tied at the bottom, white this time, appropriate for today, although some people might disagree as to whether she gets to wear white. It's her day. She can do whatever she wants, just like every day.

She makes her way to the front of the church and takes her place opposite the three of us. We move through the vows until it's time for me to say mine.

"Wendy, you already know this, but I'm committing to it in front of everyone. I will be there for you for the entirety of your life, and beyond if I can figure out how. I no longer need to be the only man for you. And I never thought I'd say that in my wedding vows. It's just proof that you're special. You make me a better person, and I'm proud to stand up here and promise to take on the role of best husband ever."

Grumblings come from my brothers, but I ramble on nervously, since this is uncharted territory for me, being in front of people, exposing myself. Apparently, I have some desire to keep her all to myself as I feel like spending the rest of my life declaring how much I love her.

Controlling my mouth, I let the ceremony continue. Knight says something about claiming his destiny. I think he's quoting the fortune. Nova talks about the 'pain of the past' making the present even brighter. I'm too lost in Wendy's eyes to process anything until the officiant says, "You may kiss the bride."

It's a natural command my body responds to. I lean forward, my brothers moving in at the same time. I know we planned this out in the rehearsal dinner, but plans don't matter anymore. We go for it. We're all in there, loving her with wild abandon in front of everyone because this is her wedding and she should get what she wants—men who truly, openly love her for herself.

And we live happily ever after!

Would you like a little more **Ribbons and Role Play**?

If you'd like more role play, grab the BONUS SCENE by signing up for my newsletter.

Once you subscribe, I'll keep you up to date on my stories, sales, and other Super Hot content you won't want to miss!

Visit my website: https://SylvieHaas.com
And true to my initials, SHhhh, I'll let it be our little secret.

More by Sylvie Haas

Eggplant Canyon
Claimed by my Ex's Dad & His Friend
Claimed by my Stepbrothers
Heat Stroked
Claimed by my Boss & His Twin
Claimed by my Best Friend's Brothers
Claimed by my Lawyers

Sugar D's Speed Dating
Why Choose the Bodyguards
Why Choose the Stepbrothers
Why Choose the Billionaires
Why Choose the Beards

Christmas Cherry Auction

Sparkles and Spankings

Presents and Praise

Tinsel and Teasing

Holidays and Handcuffs

Wishful and Wanton

Baking and Blindfolds

Carols and Consent

Sugarplums and Submission

Ribbons and Role Play

Eggplant Canyon Phase 2: The Bratva Moves In

Virgin and the Bratva

Fake Engagement and the Bratva

Secret Baby and the Bratva

and more...

About the Author

Sylvie Haas obsesses over dirty-talking heroes who fall hard and fast for the woman of their dreams. And you'll find multiple heroes in one book because she has such a hard time making the heroine choose one possessive guy.

On most days, you can find Sylvie with the wind in her hair, her fingers on the keyboard, and her mind in the gutter as she thinks up new places her characters can get frisky.

Sylvie's books will always deliver a happily ever after, and even though they're short, they'll leave you satisfied!

If you haven't signed up for her newsletter yet, there's still room. The more the merrier!

https://SylvieHaas.com